W9-AZS-482

Schaumburg Township District Library
130 South Roselle Rd.
Schaumburg, IL 60193

Dear Parents:

Congratulations! Your child is taking the first steps on an exciting journey. The destination? Independent reading!

STEP INTO READING® will help your child get there. The program offers five steps to reading success. Each step includes fun stories and colorful art or photographs. In addition to original fiction and books with favorite characters, there are Step into Reading Non-Fiction Readers, Phonics Readers and Boxed Sets, Sticker Readers, and Comic Readers—a complete literacy program with something to interest every child.

Learning to Read, Step by Step!

Ready to Read   Preschool–Kindergarten
• big type and easy words • rhyme and rhythm • picture clues
For children who know the alphabet and are eager to begin reading.

Reading with Help   Preschool–Grade 1
• basic vocabulary • short sentences • simple stories
For children who recognize familiar words and sound out new words with help.

Reading on Your Own   Grades 1–3
• engaging characters • easy-to-follow plots • popular topics
For children who are ready to read on their own.

Reading Paragraphs   Grades 2–3
• challenging vocabulary • short paragraphs • exciting stories
For newly independent readers who read simple sentences with confidence.

Ready for Chapters   Grades 2–4
• chapters • longer paragraphs • full-color art
For children who want to take the plunge into chapter books but still like colorful pictures.

STEP INTO READING® is designed to give every child a successful reading experience. The grade levels are only guides; children will progress through the steps at their own speed, developing confidence in their reading.

Remember, a lifetime love of reading starts with a single step!

For my parents,
who encouraged me
to roam. —L.M.

Step into Reading, Random House, and the Random House colophon are registered trademarks of Penguin Random House LLC.

Visit us on the Web!
StepIntoReading.com
randomhousekids.com

Educators and librarians, for a variety of teaching tools, visit us at RHTeachersLibrarians.com

ISBN 978-0-7364-3802-5 (trade) — ISBN 978-0-7364-9018-4 (lib. bdg.)
ISBN 978-0-7364-3767-7 (ebook)

Printed in the United States of America   10 9 8 7 6 5 4 3 2 1

Ariel
IS FEARLESS

by Liz Marsham

illustrated by the
Disney Storybook Art Team

Random House 🏠 New York

One night,

Ariel hears

her sister coughing.

Andrina is very sick.
She needs a medicine
made from night lilies.

Andrina says night lilies
are guarded
by ghost lights.

Ariel is not afraid
of ghosts.

She and Flounder
leave the kingdom.
They will find
night lilies.

At the border,

they see guards.

Ariel tells Flounder

to be quiet.

The guards see
small blue lights.
The ghost lights!

Ariel and Flounder swim

toward the lights.

Flounder is scared.
He thinks the lights
are a shark!
Ariel tells him
not to worry.

The lights are
not sharks.

They are not ghosts.

They are
a school of fish!
They swim above
the night lilies.

The fish are lost!
One fish asks
Ariel and Flounder
for help.

They need
to find the shore.
They need
to find their family.

Ariel brings the fish
to the surface.
She points
to a star.

If the fish
follow the star,
they will find
the shore.

The fish thank Ariel.

They swim away.

A few minutes later,
the guards see
more lights.
Ghost lights!

It is not
ghost lights
that they see.
They see Ariel
and Flounder!

They have night lilies.

The flowers are glowing.

They will bring

the flowers to Andrina.

Thanks to Ariel,
Andrina gets better!
She tells everyone
about her brave sister.

The people love
the new market.
And Jasmine loves
helping the people!

Dear Parents:

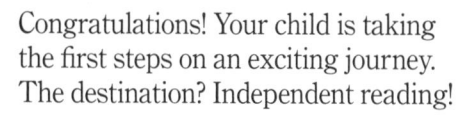

Congratulations! Your child is taking the first steps on an exciting journey. The destination? Independent reading!

STEP INTO READING® will help your child get there. The program offers five steps to reading success. Each step includes fun stories and colorful art or photographs. In addition to original fiction and books with favorite characters, there are Step into Reading Non-Fiction Readers, Phonics Readers and Boxed Sets, Sticker Readers, and Comic Readers—a complete literacy program with something to interest every child.

Learning to Read, Step by Step!

Ready to Read   Preschool–Kindergarten
• big type and easy words • rhyme and rhythm • picture clues
For children who know the alphabet and are eager to begin reading.

Reading with Help   Preschool–Grade 1
• basic vocabulary • short sentences • simple stories
For children who recognize familiar words and sound out new words with help.

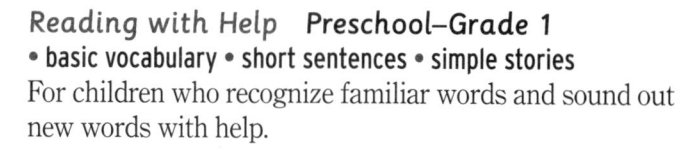

Reading on Your Own   Grades 1–3
• engaging characters • easy-to-follow plots • popular topics
For children who are ready to read on their own.

Reading Paragraphs   Grades 2–3
• challenging vocabulary • short paragraphs • exciting stories
For newly independent readers who read simple sentences with confidence.

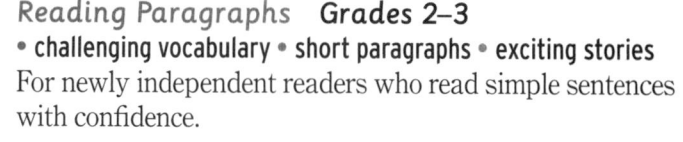

Ready for Chapters   Grades 2–4
• chapters • longer paragraphs • full-color art
For children who want to take the plunge into chapter books but still like colorful pictures.

STEP INTO READING® is designed to give every child a successful reading experience. The grade levels are only guides; children will progress through the steps at their own speed, developing confidence in their reading.

Remember, a lifetime love of reading starts with a single step!

For Emilia
—S.F.

Step into Reading, Random House, and the Random House colophon are registered trademarks of Penguin Random House LLC.

Visit us on the Web!
StepIntoReading.com
randomhousekids.com

Educators and librarians, for a variety of teaching tools, visit us at RHTeachersLibrarians.com

ISBN 978-0-7364-3802-5 (trade) — ISBN 978-0-7364-9018-4 (lib. bdg.)
ISBN 978-0-7364-3767-7 (ebook)

Printed in the United States of America   10 9 8 7 6 5 4 3 2 1

DISNEY PRINCESS

Jasmine
IS HELPFUL

by Suzanne Francis

illustrated by the
Disney Storybook Art Team

Random House 🏠 New York

Princess Jasmine
is tired
of palace life.
She wants to go
outside the palace walls.
So does Rajah.

Jasmine sees Jafar
taking letters
from her father.

He says they are
silly letters
from the people
of the kingdom.

Jasmine wants
to read the letters.
Her father says no.

He tells her
to go to the garden
and be a proper princess.

Jasmine is upset.

She wants to do more

for her kingdom.

Rajah has a surprise.
He gives her one
of the letters.

Jasmine reads the letter.
A man says the market
is falling apart.

Jasmine wants
to see the market.
She tries
to climb the wall.
It is too high.

Jasmine has an idea.

She uses a scarf
to climb.

Rajah helps.

Jasmine reaches
the top of the wall.
She looks
at the market.

It *is* old
and falling apart.

Jasmine tells her father about the market.

He says she should not have climbed the wall.

Jasmine does
not give up.

She wants to help.

She reads more letters
about the market.

Jasmine tells her father
and Jafar
she wants to build
a new market.

Jafar says no.

Jasmine says she will

use her jewels

to pay for it.

The sultan
loves the idea.
He says yes.

Now Jasmine is
in charge
of reading letters.